The Ornament

by

Michael A. Galitello

ISBN: 9781073732340
Published By Ivory Pearl Publications

Dedication

The Ornament is dedicated to all the children in the world
who dream, who hope, who believe

Acknowledgments

I want to thank Andrea Antczak and her daughter Lia for their careful reading of the manuscript in its final stages and their thoughtful comments about the story. Their help is much appreciated.

So too is the help of Luca Gebhart and her interest in the book and her comments about it.

Romy, your encouragement for me to write the book is rewarded, as you know, in the name of the main character.

My thanks also go to Shaya Riddick for her help in the choice of the cover images.

Finally, I want to thank my ghostwriter Rob Carr for once again helping me bring my dreams to life.

Chapter One

"What will daddy look like?" Romy asked her mother.

"I'm sure he'll look just like he did when he left," her mother answered, but Romy could see she really wasn't sure herself. "It's only been a year," her mother added.

"It seems like forever," Romy said.

The first snowflake of the Christmas season floated down and landed on the tip of twelve year old Romy's nose.

"That's good luck!" Tamika, her best friend, whispered to her.

Romy knew she was having good luck today. Her dad -- and Tamika's -- was arriving back at Fort Drum, New York, from a year long tour of duty in the Middle East, a year without a whole family, Romy thought.

Tamika stuck her tongue out into the cool December air and began weaving her head back and forth. Finally she landed her own snowflake on the tip of her tongue.

She turned to Romy and the two girls gave each other high fives, dark hand to light hand high in the air.

"You're magic," Romy said in her usual throaty voice. She sounded like a girl much older. Her blond hair swayed back and forth as she moved her head as she now tried to catch a snowflake on her tongue, too.

Suddenly the crowd standing all around them on the edge of the tarmac went silent. The heavy whoosh of jet engines braking on the runway behind them prompted every head to turn and look behind them as the huge airliner set down.

Each heart in the group of two hundred beat a little faster in anticipation of seeing a husband, a son, a father, a boyfriend who hadn't been seen, hadn't been held, in a year.

Romy and her mother had become close while her father was away, but despite the e-mail, Skyping and letters, Romy realized her father had become a little unreal to her, a little too distant.

The plane landed and taxied around at the end of the runway. As the crowd turned to watch, their heads moved in unison, like a flock of birds moving together in one pattern in the sky, as their eyes followed the silver craft around and then back down the runway until it stopped in front of them.

The plane's metal door opened and a stairway was rolled up to the side of the plane. Romy, Tamika and their moms stood up on their tippy toes. They were at the front of the crowd and there was no one in front of them, but they were so excited to get their first look at their dads, Brad and Vance, that they could no longer keep their feet flat on the ground.

Jenny and Pam, their mothers, stood right behind the girls with their hands across the top of their daughters' shoulders. They wanted to comfort the girls, but they also needed to steady themselves.

"This is like a first date, isn't it?" Jenny giggled in Pam's ear.

Their mothers hands felt comforting on the girls shoulders, but Romy and Tamika were both wide-eyed with the excitement of seeing their fathers.

"Is your skin tingling?" Romy asked Tamika.

Tamika was too excited to speak. She nodded her head up and down quickly and rubbed a hand across her dark cheek, as if trying to wipe the tingles away.

"Me, too!" Romy said.

As the soldiers started coming out through the door of the plane in their tan camouflage uniforms and blood red berets, the girls scanned each face as one soldier after another came down the stairs.

"What if I can't recognize my dad?" Romy asked Tamika.

"They've all got name tags on their chests, silly," Tamika said. "See?" and she pointed at one of the soldiers with her finger.

And what if he doesn't recognize me, Romy, suddenly wondered, and she felt her stomach sink. My hair's so much longer, she thought, I'm taller, and my voice is so different. Maybe he won't know me. I'm not a little kid any more.

The men from the 10th Mountain Division walked in an orderly line across the tarmac, but as soon as they neared the crowd, they broke into running until each held his family tight within his arms.

Tamika was the first to spot her father. He appeared in the doorway and right behind him was Romy's dad. Both girls started waving frantically, but neither father could make out his own daughter among the sea of waving arms in front of them. Brad paused on the top stair, squinted and focused his eyes on the weaving crowd, but he still couldn't recognize his daughter Romy.

When Brad and Vance had reached the bottom of the stairs and started across the tarmac, Jenny and Pam released their daughters' shoulders and the two girls ran to their dads.

The four of them came together like magnets and disappeared into each other's arms, father and daughter, father and daughter, hugging as if they were one.

After a long minute, Romy peeked around under her father's arm at Tamika, enveloped within her own father's strong arms. Romy looked up at Vance's face. He seemed to be smiling, but his eyes were shut so tight Romy thought it must hurt, and then she saw a tear squeeze out from under his eyelid and glide down his cheek.

She realized her own face was now covered in tears, too, but her cheeks actually hurt from smiling so much. We're family again, she thought, as she felt her fathers arms around her.

Jenny had caught Pam's arm by the elbow when she first had started to follow her daughter out onto the tarmac.

"Let's let the girls have their fill," she said.

"Good idea," Pam said and paused in her step.

Now, as Brad and Vance held their daughters at arm's length to look into their faces, Jenny and Pam started out onto the tarmac. Romy looked closely into her father's face. He had a new moustache, thick and dark, and she strained trying to recognize the familiar face that she had known underneath it.

Soon the mothers were each tight in their husband's arms, the tears flowing down their cheeks.

"C'mon, girls. Finish those Danish," Pam said to Tamika and Romy. "We've got to get you two over to the mall. There's only two weeks left for you to finish your Christmas shopping, you know."

"Yeah," Jenny added, "we want to make sure you have plenty of time to get us something really nice."

The four of them were finishing their weekly brunch at Panera's, where they'd been going for their Saturday morning treat every weekend since the girls' fathers had been away.

Brad and Vance still had to work until two every Saturday at the Orleans post office. They'd been there since they graduated together from high school, both local basketball stars, and Kevin Shaughnessy, the postmaster, Jenny's great uncle, had been holding their jobs for them while they were away on military duty.

"Mom, can I have a sip of your coffee before we go?" Tamika asked.

"Now, honey, what kind of a mom would I be if I let my twelve year old daughter have caffeine?"

"The best kind!" Tamika yelled out.

"See. You're already wired," Pam said. "No. Now let's get out of here."

After their mothers dropped them off at the mall, Romy and Tamika made a beeline to Michael's Jewelers. The week before they had seen two little silver lockets on thin chains which opened with a tiny clasp to put a picture in. The girls had already decided they'd get them for their mothers, and today they had their money with them.

"Your mothers will love these," the young sales clerk said to them. "Did you know there's a photo booth down on Level A where you can get some little portraits of yourself to stick inside?"

"Really? Cool," Tamika said.

After they'd taken sixteen pictures each, giggling loudly at all their efforts to look beautiful for their mothers, they went over to the food court to look through the photos and decide the best ones to put into the lockets.

The girls sat and sipped their hot chocolate and sorted through the photos, laughing at the ones that looked too silly and contemplating the two or three that looked like their mothers would like them. After much back and forth between them, they finally agreed on the best one for each of their lockets.

"They're going to love these!" Tamika said.

"But what are we going to get our dads?" Romy asked.

The girls stared at each other blankly for a minute.

"We can't do lockets for them?" Tamika joked.

"Nah. They've already got dog tags," Romy said and thought for a second. "Seriously, what are we going to get them? They've got everything, don't they?"

"I know. Every guy thing, anyway."

Romy was still thinking. "Tamika, did you ever worry about your dad when he was gone?"

"Sure. Some dads don't come back."

"So what can we get them to show them we're glad they did?" Romy asked.

"We don't even know who they are any more, do we," Tamika said. "I mean, maybe they've changed a lot."

"Maybe," Romy said. "It's almost like a different family now, isn't it?"

The two girls ate silently, fingering their mothers' lockets, and sipped the last of their hot chocolate.

"Well, at least we've got our mom's covered," Tamika finally said.

"Yes, we do!" Romy said as the two girls stood.

Tamika slipped her arm through Romy's and the two of them marched off together out into the main mall from the food court, their mothers' lockets and their photos secure in the pretty little shopping bags on each of the girl's arms.

Standing outside on the curb in front of the main entrance to the mall, waiting for their mothers, Romy and Tamika each held their two hands out in front of them to catch the tiniest of snow flakes, like little white wafers, now falling from the sky.

Chapter Two

Romy looked at Tamika's face staring out at her from her computer screen. The two girls were Skyping after school as they did every day when they weren't together at either Romy's or Tamika's house.

"So, really, what are we going to get our dads for Christmas?" Romy asked.

"What does your dad say he wants?" Tamika asked.

"Not a tie. What's yours say?"

"A Hummer. I've got $32.78 saved so far. Don't think I'll make it by Christmas," Tamika said.

"Yeah, he's like my dad, not much help either. What's your mom getting him?"

"Not a tie. Yours?

"Not a Hummer."

"So what are we going to do?" Romy asked.

Suddenly the screen in front of Romy went all white and snowy.

Surprised, Romy looked into the vibrating blizzard of white particles on her monitor and clicked her mouse with her index finger, trying to restore the image of Tamika. The longer she stared into the snowy screen, the fuzzier she herself felt.

Tamika's computer, too, had gone all snowy. She stared at all the little white particles, kept clicking her mouse, turned her screen on and off and then pounded her desk to try to restore Romy's image. Nothing worked.

Tamika decided just to wait it out, and she sat there silently staring into the snowy screen feeling frustrated and a little dazed.

Soon Romy heard the front doorbell ring and she called out through the open door of her room, “Dad, are you getting that?”

“Yep. I got it,” her father called back.

Romy heard her father open the heavy front door and then heard soft male voices speaking. She couldn’t make out anything that was being said, but they talked for a long time.

Romy finally got up from her desk and walked over to peek out her window. There was a police car parked in front of their house.

Startled, she walked back over to her desk and sat down, just in time to hear the front door shut. Her monitor screen was still all snowy. She thought she could hear her father crying in the living room, but she wasn’t sure. She’d never heard him cry before.

Should I go out there or should I just leave him alone, she thought to herself. Maybe something bad happened at the post office. Maybe somebody died.

She wanted to go find out, but she didn't want to embarrass her father. He'd probably feel funny if she saw him and he was crying.

She sat at her desk, waiting, trying to figure out what she should do.

After several minutes her father appeared at her door. She could see he really had been crying, but his eyes were dry now and he looked sad. Sad and serious. He had a little shopping bag in his hands, like the one Romy had with her mother's locket in it, which she'd hidden in her bottom drawer under her sweaters.

"Romy," he said, "there's been an accident."

"Who was it?" she asked.

"Your mother. And Tamika's. At the entrance to the mall. A truck went out of control. They didn't make it."

Romy burst into tears.

"Mommy!" she cried out.

"I am so sorry, Romy," her father said as he pulled her into his arms.

When Romy's crying had turned to sobbing, her father let her step back from him and he opened the little bag.

"The policeman gave me this. It was all they found, except her purse," he said.

Romy looked at the bag and felt as though a cold wind was moving through her chest.

Her father reached in and pulled out a silver charm bracelet with a little dolphin, a polar bear, a hummingbird, a unicorn and the four silver letters, R O M Y, all hanging from the polished silver band.

"I think it was your Christmas present," Brad said. "She knew how much you and Tamika love animals."

"Does Tamika know?" Romy asked.

"Sergeant Nelson -- you know him, from the Y -- is on his way to her house next. They found an identical bracelet for her."

That night, while her father was out getting them pizza, as neither of them was in a mood to cook, Romy walked around the dark house thinking about her mother. Romy didn't want any lights on because as she walked, she wanted to feel close to her mother by imagining her in the living room vacuuming, in the kitchen cooking or in her bedroom reading stories while cuddled up on the bed next to Romy. As she walked slowly through the dark house, she began to feel her mother's presence more and more.

She suddenly remembered her snowy computer screen

"I know you tried to contact me this afternoon," Romy whispered as she walked back into the living room from the kitchen. She walked over to the picture of her mom on the mantle and stood in front of it, looking into her mom's face, eye to eye.

"I know you wanted to tell me I would be okay, but you couldn't get through the snow on my computer screen. I know I'll be okay, mom, but I want to say good-bye to you. I want to give you your Christmas present."

Romy walked over to the Christmas tree that she, her mom and her dad had set up and decorated the Sunday before. The ornaments were all carefully hung, the tinsel glistened, even in the dark room, and an angel oversaw all from her perch on the top of the tree's nettled spine.

For the first time in hours, Romy's chest no longer felt chilled.

Suddenly Romy noticed a silver ornament hanging on the tree which she'd never seen before. She knew they hadn't hung it that Sunday. She walked up close to it – it was right at her eye level – and she looked into the face of Santa which was painted delicately on the ornament.

To the left of his smiling face, under the Northern Lights, was a range of snow covered mountains. To his right, under the North Star, was a similar array of white peaks. Below him a white snowfield spanned the distance between the two mountain ranges.

Romy stared at the Christmas bulb in surprise. As her eyes adjusted to the dim light of the living room, she began to make out the two inscriptions on it.

In a semicircle across the top of the ornament were the words "If you need me, I am here" and the words continued across the bottom with "at the land of ice and snow, the land where mountains glow. Believe."

"The land of ice and snow. The land where mountains glow," Romy repeated in a whisper. She wondered where that could be and then whispered again, "If you need me, I am here."

She stood there silently in the dark next to the tree, rolling all this over in her mind for a minute.

"Santa, I need you," she whispered.

Her father came back home with the pizza and they sat down at the kitchen table to eat. Somehow, to Romy, the hard surface of the Formica table, all by itself in the middle of the room, made the kitchen seem so much more lonely, not like she'd ever seen it before. Her mother had always brought life to the room.

Romy and her father ate without interest, without talking, her dad lost in his own thoughts, Romy wondering where the land of ice, snow and glowing mountains was.

"I'm going to my room, I think," Romy said to her dad after the two of them had cleaned up the table and set the box of leftover pizza slices on a shelf in the fridge. Neither of them had been very hungry.

"That's fine, sweetheart," Brad said. "Are you okay?

"No, but I'll be okay," Romy said. "You?"

"I don't know," he said. "It's hard."

"I know," Romy said and went over to him, stood on her tip toes and kissed him on his cheek before she went to her room. The bristles of his moustache had scratched her cheek.

"Night, dad. Love you."

"Love you too."

In her room Romy turned her computer on, happy to find it was working again. She clicked to Google and started looking for maps of all the areas within the Arctic Circle and up toward the North Pole where "glowing" mountains might be.

She saw that there was no actual land at the North Pole, just ice that shifted around in the cold waters at the top of the globe. The closest land was Peary Land off the northern tip of Greenland.

She Googled Greenland and found one site with a three dimensional rendering of the deep glacier that formed the center of the island. The ice field ran from north to south, but east to west it spanned the distance between two tall mountain chains.

Just like the picture on the ornament, Romy thought.

She should go to Greenland, she realized, and Santa would help her give her mom the locket. She believed.

Wait, she thought. I can bring my dad and we can both say good-bye to mom. That'll be his Christmas present!

She played with her new idea, back and forth, comfortably, in her mind, pleased with how perfect it would all be.

And Tamika can bring her dad, too!

She reached for her phone and dialed Tamika.

"Hi, Romy," Tamika answered quietly.

The two girls had talked by phone earlier that afternoon, after the police had left Tamika's, and had cried together until they just couldn't cry any more.

Now Romy could tell how exhausted, how limp, Tamika was.

"You know, we've got to go to Greenland," Romy told her. There was no doubt in her voice.

"What?"

"Go see if there's a new ornament on your Christmas tree."

"What?"

"Just go do it, Tamika. I'll wait."

In a minute she heard Tamika's voice again. "Romy, what is that?" She described an ornament identical to the one Romy had found on her tree.

"We've just got to go to Greenland," Romy repeated and told her how she figured out that was the land of ice and snow where the mountains glow. "Santa will help us say good-bye to our moms. And our dads, too. That's what we're going to give them for Christmas! It'll be perfect!"

"Are you sure?"

"Santa says 'If you need me, I am here.' Why else would he have given us these ornaments?"

"How do you know he gave them to us?"

"Well, who else would, silly?"

"Daddy, we've got to go to Greenland," Romy declared to her father the next morning.

Tamika and her dad had come over with donuts and coffee and the four of them sat at the kitchen table. Both girls had shown their fathers the ornaments they'd found on their Christmas trees.

"You know, so we can say good-bye to mom," Romy added. "I've got to give mom her locket for Christmas, too. Tamika, you and your dad too."

"What?" Brad said.

His face looked surprised, but a little frightened, Romy noticed. This might be too much for him, she thought. Maybe it was too soon.

"Santa's going to help us say good-bye to our moms," Romy said again, more confidently. "We can get to him by going right up the center of Greenland to the North Pole. I Googled it."

Brad looked over at Vance as if he wanted help of some kind, but wasn't sure just what kind.

"Well, Romy," Vance said, "I think that might be a good idea, honey, but I don't know that we can go right now. Brad and I have to get back to work in a couple days. This is the busiest time of the year for us, you know. And, I don't know about you, Brad," Vance looked over at his friend, seeking some agreement, "but I don't have the extra cash at the moment to spring for a trip to Greenland. You?"

"No," Brad said. "This is an expensive time of year. Besides, doesn't Santa have all those presents to be getting ready for the kids? He might be a little too busy to see us."

Romy saw the doubt in the two fathers' faces. She knew she had to say something very clever, very fast.

"Don't you believe in Santa?" she asked her dad.

All four of them could felt the sudden silence.

Finally Brad spoke. "Well, you know, it's not, uh, so much a question of that, but it's, really, more like, uh, how do we know Santa will have the time to help us?"

"Because he was the one who sent us those ornaments," Romy declared.

Gotcha, she thought.

Brad looked across the table at Vance and the two men stared at each other in silence.

Romy noticed out the kitchen window that snowflakes had started to fall again and she felt the kitchen seemed brighter again inside, somehow.

Chapter Three

The next morning Romy was finishing up a large bowl of Cap'n Crunch at the kitchen table while her father picked at a piece of toast which was now cold.

"Dad?" she said. She wanted to make sure she had his attention.

"Yes?"

"You know we do have to go to the North Pole, don't you?"

"Romy…" he said, not quite angry, but on the verge.

"We've got to say good-bye to mommy and I've got to give her the locket I got her for Christmas. Tamika has one for her mom, too."

"Now, Romy. I love that you want to say good-bye to mom…"

"Not just me. You, too," Romy interrupted.

She was on a mission and that mission included her dad.

"Right. And I know you and Tamika want to give them the lockets."

He paused. Romy knew he was trying to be as nice as he could while he told her they weren't going to be able to go.

"But I don't think we can go. You're basically out of school for the holidays, but Vance and I have to go back to work in a couple days. Neither of us have the money to go to the North Pole anyway. This just isn't the time to go. Maybe next year."

"Next year's too late, dad. We've got to go now. Mom's waiting. I'm sure. And Santa will help us."

"Now, about Santa Claus…" Romy's dad began.

"I know! Isn't it amazing he left us those ornaments? And he's going to help us get there. I can't wait."

"I really don't know where that ornament came from, Romy, but…"

"Dad. Last night I Googled how to get to the North Pole. It's simple. We drive up to Ottawa, catch a flight to Iqaluit up the Nunavut Province, and from there it's a short hop over to Nuuk on Greenland Airways. We hire a couple dog sleds and head north across Greenland. Mom's with Santa, I know. Tamika's mom, too."

"Honey, I don't have that kind of money at the moment. Or that kind of time."

Romy could see her dad felt relieved that he had the two perfect excuses not to go, time and money.

Suddenly there was a knock on the front door. Brad went out to the living room to see who was there.

Romy poured herself another bowl of Cap'n Crunch.

When her father came back into the kitchen several minutes later, he had a look on his face that Romy had never seen before.

"What's wrong, dad?" she asked him.

"That was Kevin, you know, my boss. He told me how sorry all the guys at work were for us, and he told me to take off work until the beginning of the year. Tamika's dad, too."

"Wow," Romy said. Things are looking up, she thought.

Her father held up a crumpled paper lunch bag he'd been holding in his right hand.

"And look at this," he said.

He still had the oddest expression on his face.

He reached into the bag and started pulling out handfuls of green bills and stacking them on the kitchen table.

"Almost five thousand dollars," he said. "The guys took up a collection."

Well, so much for time and money, she thought. Thank you, Santa.

"Then we can go!" Romy shouted out. Things really were looking up. Romy looked around the kitchen. There was no doubt it really was getting brighter.

"Well, now honey, you know, it's not quite that simple."

Sure it is, Romy thought, but she knew she had more work to do -- she and Santa -- to convince him they absolutely had to make the trip.

It was time to call Tamika.

But why isn't it snowing, Romy wondered, as she looked out the kitchen window. She wasn't sure why, but she knew they needed snowflakes.

"I think I'm making progress with my dad," Tamika said to Romy as the two girls snuggled up on their beds with their phones.

"Really? How'd you do that?" Romy asked.

"I told him that if we didn't go, we knew we would never be able to say good-bye to mom. If we went – or at least tried to go – we knew we at least had a chance."

"That's pretty good, Tamika," Romy said.

"My dad's real logical," Tamika said. "He likes those kinds of arguments."

"My dad's not that logical. He's more of a 'from your gut' kinda guy."

"Then maybe you should just cry and sob and throw a huge tantrum."

"Maybe…" Romy said, thinking about that for a moment. "Nah. That'd make him feel bad. He feels bad enough already. I think it's the Santa thing."

"What d'ya mean, 'the Santa thing'?" Tamika asked.

"Does your dad believe in Santa?'

Uh…I don't think so."

"Mine neither. But if he thinks I do – we do – he won't want us to be disappointed by going up to the North Pole and not finding Santa, let alone not finding mom. He'll want to protect us from that. 'Cause he thinks it won't happen. Your dad, too."

"You're right," Tamika said. "So what do we do?"

"I think I know," Romy said.

"Really?"

"You believe in Santa, right?" Romy asked her friend.

"Of course. Where do you think those ornaments came from?" Tamika asked.

"Exactly. So I need to talk to Santa," Romy said. "Just like mom talked to me, before I found the ornament."

"Then say hello to Santa for me, too, please," Tamika said quietly.

Romy looked out the window of her own bedroom, happy now to see the first snowflakes of the evening beginning to fall. She began to talk to Santa.

Later that night Romy heard the phone ring and tiptoed to her bedroom door and opened it a crack so she could hear her father answer it.

"Hi, Brad," she heard.

"You've got to be kidding!" came next. "I'd never even heard of Iqaluit until Romy told me that was how we'd get to Greenland," he said. "When are they going?"

Romy was straining so hard to hear every word through the slit in her door that she thought her ear would pop inside out.

"The girls will certainly think that's perfect," Vance said. "Brad, let me ask you. Are you really thinking about going?"

There was a long silence and Vance finally said, "Yeah, I guess I am. I just worry about them being disappointed."

There was more silence.

"Yeah, I know, I know. If we don't let them try, we'll never know, and that'll be even worse for them. And, no, I don't know any more than you do about where those two ornaments came from. It's spooky."

Vance paused, and Romy almost felt she could hear him thinking.

"Okay, I'm in," he said finally.

Yes! Romy pumped her right fist in the air and then threw an imaginary high five somewhere up toward Santa.

"Romy!" her father called out to her after he'd hung up the receiver.

Romy had to pull down on both of her cheeks with the palms of her hands just to wipe off the excitement she knew was showing there, as well as the grin that she knew stretched across her face.

"Yes, dad. Just a second."

She went into the kitchen and sat down at the kitchen table across form her father. She tried wrinkling her brow so she would look more serious.

"Two of Brad's friends, Army pilots at Fort Drum, have to fly a cargo plane up to Iqaluit tomorrow. They wanted to know if Brad, Tamika, you and I want to ride with them. Said it might help us take our minds off things."

Brad looked at his daughter expectantly. She knew he was hoping she'd say no, but she saw too that he knew she'd say yes.

"That would be convenient," she said, as composed as she could make herself. "We'd only have to take that little hop over to Nuuk then."

"Right."

Her dad looked at her across the table.

"This doesn't seem at all…well, weird to you?" he asked her.

"No, dad. You and I have got to say good-bye to mom. I've got to give her that locket. That's not weird. That's normal. She's waiting for us. Santa too."

"I see," her dad said, but Romy could tell he didn't see at all.

"I'll start packing," Romy said. She started to get up from the table and asked him, "Do you need any help packing, dad?"

"No, honey. I think I'll be alright. I'll call Vance and tell him we're going."

"Those pilots will be pretty surprised, won't they," Romy said, "when we tell them we're not coming back down here with them from Iqaluit."

"Yes, honey. They'll be pretty surprised."

Her father had gotten up and was walking around the kitchen, wandering really, Romy thought, until he finally went over and looked out the back window.

"It's snowing pretty good out there now, Romy. Hope it doesn't cancel our flight tomorrow."

"Oh, it won't, dad."

Early the next morning the silver cargo plane rose into the sky from Fort Drum and headed northeast. As it climbed higher and higher, the silver wings and fuselage began to glimmer with the light from the sun, now rising in front of them.

Romy looked out her window and could see a blanket of dark clouds stretched out to the west behind them, but ahead she saw nothing but clear sky. Dang, she thought. She would rather be following the snow up there.

"Three hours and we'll be in Iqaluit," she yelled to Tamika, sitting on the web backed aluminum chair beside her. There were only four seats in the front of the large cargo space. She and Tamika were together on the left, their fathers, who had almost immediately fallen asleep, were sitting to their right.

"I wonder how cold it'll be," Tamika asked, shouting.

"Once it was sixty-five below zero," Romy yelled back. "Fahrenheit."

"You've really researched all this, haven't you" Tamika asked.

Romy nodded. She looked directly at Tamika and mouthed each word with an exaggerated movement of her lips and mouth: "At least there should be a lot of snow on the ground up there."

Tamika raised her thumb in the air for an okay, tired of trying to yell over the noise of the jet engines echoing through the large open cargo space.

They sat in silence, peering out the window, watching the snow covered rock and wide rolling landscape of Quebec Province passing below them. Fir trees, such a dark green that they looked black, peppered the snowy white landscape as far as the girls' eyes could see.

The landscape below seemed so bleak. Romy thought of her mom and for a moment was sad in her heart.

She watched out the window as the earth seemed to pass below them, even though she knew it was the plane that was passing over the earth. It was like a little illusion, the thought, and soon her mind began tingling again with the excitement of the adventure they were on.

She knew they were flying ever northward to the Arctic Circle and, eventually, to the North Pole, and she knew they'd meet Santa. And mom.

Merry Christmas, dad, she thought.

Chapter Four

As they continued to fly north toward Iqaluit, Romy noticed that even though it was getting later in the day, the sun never rose much beyond where she'd first seen it at dawn. She remembered that the Arctic Circle itself – courtesy again of her nimble fingers Googling – was the point at each solstice when there was one day each year completely dark, in the winter, and one completely light, in the summer.

It suddenly dawned on her they were only a few days away from the winter solstice. They'd be far north of the Arctic Circle as they sledded north across Greenland to find the North Pole and they'd be travelling mostly in the dark.

She shuddered. She liked the daylight better. I'm only a little scared of the dark, she told herself. It'll be okay, though, because the night doesn't bother Tamika at all.

Still, Romy realized her normal world would be, well, she thought, like completely upside down.

She heard the engines of the large plane slow a bit and she felt the plane begin to descend. Soon she could see a large bright yellow block building in the distance, the Iquluit airport terminal. There were no longer any trees this far north and in the middle of the snow and rock filled landscape the bright yellow terminal of the Iqaluit airport looked like a huge Lego building some enormous child had erected there.

Things here really did look, maybe not exactly upside down, but all unexpected, all opposite, Romy thought again. It was a different world up here.

Romy and Tamika stood on the snow covered tarmac, shivering and huddled up together, as their dads told the Air Force pilots they wouldn't be returning with them that afternoon. Romy watched as Peter, one of the pilots, threw his arms up in the air, frustrated he couldn't talk Brad into flying the girls back home with him. Romy knew Peter's daughter in school, and Romy could see he thought it was just way too dangerous up here for two young girls.

Romy hoped he was wrong.

Peter turned abruptly and walked away from Brad, but Vance and the other pilot shook hands and then Vance and Brad walked back over to the girls.

"Well, they certainly were surprised," Vance said. "Especially Peter."

"More than surprised, I'd say," Brad added. "Let's get inside the terminal, get warm and get our tickets for Nuuk."

Romy and Tamika looked at each other, a little guilt in their eyes. They knew Brad was not happy and suspected Vance might not be either.

This was going to be some trip, Romy thought, as they entered the warmth of the yellow building.

As their little two engine plane descended into Nuuk, Greenland, it was already dusk, even though it was only two o'clock in the afternoon.

The low sun had just set, but there was still enough light for the girls to see the collection of red, green, yellow and blue houses and buildings that made up Nuuk, nestled under the base of Sermitsiag Mountain. Here too it looked to Romy like some enormous child had been at play building these brightly colored houses in the middle of the snowy landscape.

Maybe it has something to do with getting so close to Santa's village, Romy thought.

"This town looks like it was built by Santa's elves," Romy whispered to Tamika.

"That's a good sign, isn't it?" Tamika asked.

Romy nodded her head, but still felt a little of the guilt she had felt at the airport in Iqaluit for dragging her father up into this frozen, fairy tale land.

That night in the living room of their two bedroom hotel suite in the Nordbo hotel, itself a long, low, bright red structure, Romy and Tamika were going over with their fathers their plans for flying up to Ilulisset the next morning to hire the sleds and dog teams that would take all of them north to find Santa.

"You know, Brad and I have been thinking," Tamika's father said when the girls had finished talking. "We've looked at all the possibilities and it seems that it must have been your mothers who put those ornaments on our trees."

Wow, Tamika's right, Romy thought. He is pretty logical.

"So, assuming that's the case," Vance went on, "we just want to tell you girls how proud we are of you for trying to make this trip, but it's probably time for us to end our adventure. We don't want to end up on some glacial snowfield, freezing to death in the dark, now do we? We can stay a few days here in Nuuk, but then Brad and I think it'll be time to go back and celebrate Christmas, comfortably, in our own homes."

Yup, logical, Romy thought. But no faith. He didn't believe.

"There was no ornament on our tree when mommy died," Tamika said. "I know. I had just finished throwing the last of the tinsel on the tree before Romy and I Skyped each other the afternoon of the accident, just before our computers went off.

By then, mom had already been out of the house shopping with Romy's mom for hours."

Romy was nodding her head in agreement.

"Well, maybe you just didn't notice it earlier," Brad said.

"We know," both girls spit out in unison.

"Mommy wants to say good-bye to us," Romy said to her father. "To you and to me. Tamika's mom too. Don't you want to say good-be to mom?"

Romy looked like she was close to crying, even though her voice sounded strong.

"Of course I do," Brad said.

Tamika was right about that sobbing tactic, Romy thought.

Now Vance was nodding his head in agreement with Brad.

Brad looked over at Vance, who looked back at him and shrugged his shoulders ever so slightly.

"Okay," Brad said. "We'll fly up to whatever it's called…"

"Ilulisset," Romy said.

"...Ilulisset in the morning."

Romy and Tamika smiled at each other and Tamika got up and walked over to the living room window. She pulled back the heavy drapes that helped keep the warmth in the cozy room.

"OMG!" she shouted.

The others got up and went over to the window and pulled the thick drapes completely back so they could all see the magical display in front of them.

The most delicate of colored celestial curtains, all greens and pinks and reds, slowly moved back and forth in waves, high up into the night sky in front of them, as if someone were spraying dancing lights across the heavens.

The four watched in amazement. A bright, full moon sat low in the horizon to the east, like a fifth observer.

"My God," Brad whispered. "The Aurora Borealis. Beautiful."

Romy noticed the tiniest of snowflakes were gently falling from on high.

"Up here," Romy said, "they call those lights the polar spirits."

The slim red Air Greenland plane made its way north along the coast the next morning from Nuuk to Ilulisset. The world was still dark, but out the window to the east Romy could see the great white ice field in the center of Greenland aglow in the light from the nearly full moon, which, like the sun at this time of the year, barely rose above the horizon. Behind the rocky peaks of the coastal mountains, the snow field stretched for as far as Romy could see to the east and the north.

"I think we've just passed the Arctic Circle," Romy called out to Brad and Vance, sitting across the aisle from Tamika, who was sitting in the seat next to Romy.

"We're in a different world now," she yelled over to the men.

Tamika was smiling, as if she too, like Romy, knew things their fathers did not know.

Soon Tamika tapped Romy's arm and pointed to the windows on the other side of the plane. Romy stretched to look and saw the little icebergs below them, glowing in the moonlight as they floated out to sea after breaking off from the curving glacier that flowed from the mountains down past the town of Ilulisset.

"We're here," Romy whispered to Tamika.

After they landed, they took a taxi up to the Hotel Arctic, a bright red structure overlooking the bay, the glacier and the steady stream of icebergs, large and small, calving into the ocean. It was only false dawn, but there was enough light in the sky now for the four of them to see clearly.

They climbed the hotel's steps, carrying their backpacks in their hands, and walked through the heavy metal door and over to the front desk.

"We need a room for tonight and we want to hire a guide and a dog sled," Brad said to the hotel clerk.

"There are no sleds available this week," the young Inuit man told them. "It's the solstice."

Brad turned to face the girls.

"Well, that's a disappointment," he said. His face showed no signs of disappointment, though.

Romy walked right up next to the counter and stood on her tiptoes so she could address the clerk over the top of the tall counter.

"Can't you at least call one of the guides for us to talk to?" she asked. "There must be one of them you think would at least talk to us."

"Well, there's Anik," the clerk said. "Just a second."

He turned around and, his back to Romy, dialed the phone on the other counter by the back wall. Romy tried to listen to what he said to make sure he was trying to be convincing, but she couldn't hear what he was saying and, she realized, even if she had, she wouldn't understand him. He was speaking Inuit.

The clerk hung up the phone and turned back around to face Romy.

"He'll be here shortly."

The four of them settled down into the sofas in the front of the lobby, but none of them spoke as they waited.

Shortly an Inuit man dressed in a long caribou hide coat walked in through the front door. The fur inside his tall collar blended in with the curly black hair on his head and his face was tanned and so weathered, it was impossible to say how old he was.

His eyes were set deep within his cheeks and brow and were a warm, dark brown. Romy felt, as she looked across the room and into them, that she was being drawn into the dark, starry night outside.

The man looked around the lobby and then walked over to Brad who, with the others, stood up from the sofas.

"Good morning," he said. "I'm Anik."

"Good morning," Brad said and shook his hand. "I'm Brad. We're looking to hire a sled for a couple days to go north."

The Inuit looked steadily into Brad's face for a moment and then scanned the faces of the other three, one by one.

"We don't hire out now," he said. "There's at best a couple hours of sunlight here, and if you want to go further north, the world is too dark."

"Isn't it a full moon?" Romy asked him.

"She's a wise one, no?" Anik turned and said to Brad. He smiled slightly for the first time.

Romy smiled back. She liked him.

"No," Brad said. "I mean yes. My 'no' was to your 'no.'" Brad suddenly seemed confused.

"That would give us a little light, yes," Anik said. "But this is not the time of year to go. It's the solstice. We have no dogs ready. No sleds set up."

Oh dear, Romy thought. Not another logical one.

"Can I talk to you?" Romy asked him.

Anik look surprised, but followed Romy over to a corner of the room.

"You see Tamika there? She and I lost our mothers last week in a terrible accident. We never had a chance to say good-bye to them. Neither did our dads. I know this sounds strange, but Tamika and I know if we go to meet Santa, he'll help us say good-bye to our moms. Plus, we have these lockets to give them for Christmas."

She pulled a crinkled piece of white tissue paper out of her pocket and unwrapped it. She lifted the locket and held it from its silver chain for the Inuit to see.

Anik looked down at Romy. His eyes looked watery to her.

"I lost my mother and my son's mother, my wife, last year. They too had a terrible accident. Sometimes my son and I go out far north onto the glacier to talk to them their spirits. It's how we keep us a family. I don't know anything about Santa, but I know you'll be able to talk to your moms out there too. I'll take you."

As he said the last words he was already pulling a

cell phone out of his pocket and dialing a number with his thick index finger.

"Qannik?" he said, and then spoke in Inuit. Romy thought it sounded like he was giving orders, but she wished she knew what all his words meant. After a minute, he hung up.

Please, Santa, Romy prayed.

"That was my son, Qannik. He's going to get the dogs, set up two sleds with supplies for three days up and three days back, and we'll be ready to go in the morning, here, at seven o'clock, your time."

"Our time?" Brad asked. He and the others had walked over to join Anik and Romy when he saw Anik calling.

"Your time is different than our time," was all that Anik said.

"Anik?" Romy said.

"Yes, little girl?"

"May I ask you what your name means? It's such a beautiful sound."

"Anik means 'seer.'"

"And your son's name, Qannik?"

"That means 'snowflake,'" Anik told her.

"Perfect," Romy said.

Chapter Five

"Boat?" Brad asked.

His face had the same expression on it Romy had seen when she first told him they needed to go to Greenland.

Uh-oh, she thought.

"We need the boat," Anik said. He'd arrived at their hotel room right at seven, their time. "We've got to go out into the sea and up around Qaarsat so we can get to the edge of the glacier we'll need to cross to get up to the ice field. My cousin's waiting for us in his boat at the harbor. Qannik's already loaded the dogs and two sleds. We'll be there this afternoon."

I love the ocean, Romy thought, but dad only likes the sand.

"The icebergs are dangerous this time of year," Anik continued, "but it's the only way to get where we need to be to start our trip."

I don't know if I love icebergs, Romy thought to herself. She looked over at Tamika. She looked calm, but alert. So did Romy's dad.

That's strange, Romy thought. Everything really is backwards up here.

"Well, let's get going then," Brad said and slapped Vance on the back.

I think dad's gone into soldier mode, Romy thought. She'd never seen her dad like this before. He was composed, but intent, and he and Vance looked like they were almost about to enjoy this adventure.

Brad, Vance and the two girls put on their parkas and shouldered the packs they'd readied the night before for their six day journey. They closed the hotel room door behind them and followed Anik along the snow packed streets of the little town to the harbor.

A small yellow boat, part tug, part trawler, sat next to the wooden pier that jutted out into the dark waters of the harbor. They could hear the engine rumbling as they walked toward it and Qannik and Anik's cousin stepped out of the pilot's cabin together and waved at them as they approached.

The girls and their dads were breathing through their mouths with the effort of walking through the frigid morning air with their heavy packs, and little clouds of moisture hung in the air in front of their faces. Romy liked listening to the sound of their boots squeaking along the snow packed street and she felt cozy staring out at the morning through the fur lined oval of her parka's hood, tightly fastened around her face.

Here we come, she thought.

In the light from the lampposts along the sides of the dock she could make out the silhouettes of two large wooden sleds propped up against one side of the boat's tiny cabin. Then she saw the mound of fur on the boat's front deck. Two dozen sled dogs had curled up into each other and were sleeping, perfectly content and comfy in the sub zero temperatures of the early morning.

After boarding the boat, she and Tamika set their packs down and walked carefully around the cabin to the front deck and kneeled to pet the thick furred Huskies. Romy wanted to lie down and curl right up with them.

The boat's engine suddenly ripped into life and Romy felt the front end of the boat lift as the it moved out from the dock and pushed into the cold waters of the open sea. She put her arms around the nearest dog and hugged its neck, and the Husky sleepily licked the tip of her nose and her cheeks.

This is going to be such a fun trip, Romy thought, and pulled one arm away from the dog to give a high five to Tamika. She had a broad smile on her face, too, and Romy knew she was thinking the same thought. Both girls had always wanted a dog the last year, but hadn't gotten one because their dads were away. Now they had twenty-four of them. They each snuggled down into the living blanket of warm fur.

As the boat moved away from the shore and away from the lights of the tiny town, Romy's eyes adjusted to the darkness above the sea, and soon she spotted the almost full moon above the horizon behind her. She knew it would stay in the sky all day and all night during its full phase, a dim replacement for the absent sun.

Everything really was backwards and upside down up here, she thought. This was another world.

Soon her eyes were able to see the mountains behind her – "glowing" in the light of the moon, she thought, just as Santa had said on the ornament. In front of her were the icebergs and ice floes the boat was weaving through on its way out to the open sea. The ice too had a soft glow to it in the light from the rising moon.

Romy and Tamika stared out over the bow at the mysterious white shapes of the icebergs floating on the black sea in front of them.

"Look!" Tamika said. "That one looks like a horse's head."

"And way over there!" Romy responded. "Look at that really huge one. It looks like that castle at Disney World."

As the boat churned forward through the dark sea, the girls played the game of naming the shapes of the ice floats just as they had done, lying on the green summer grass in their own back yards, naming the shapes they saw in the puffy white clouds passing by in the sky above them.

This is so neat, Romy thought, feeling the warmth of the dogs next to her. Even dad has stopped being, well, "difficult," now that he and Vance have decided to put on their brave soldier faces. I'm proud of him. Maybe he does believe.

"Look at that iceberg way over there," Tamika called over to Romy above the loud throb of the engine, straining now as it pushed the boat through the rough sea. They were far enough out from the land that the waves were high and the cross current strong, and the water had begun to lap almost up to the top of the railing next to the girls as the rolling sea pushed against the boat.

"That one's really humongous!" Romy shouted back to Tamika.

"It looks just like one huge wall of ice from here," Tamika yelled.

Romy squinted to get a better look at it. The spray from the waves hitting the bow of the boat splashed thousands of little pellets of water against her face and she could feel the sting of the salt as some drops hit her in the eye.

"That's not an iceberg!" she yelled to Tamika. "That's a wall of fog!"

Romy suddenly heard the men yelling at each other from inside the boat's cabin and then she felt her father's hand on her shoulder. He motioned for her to come with him and she and Tamika grabbed his strong arm as they followed him slowly back to the rear deck.

The sea had suddenly become violent, and as Romy glanced back over her shoulder, she saw the huge white wall of fog coming down on them. It must be the front of a storm, she thought, and then she felt the damp frigid air enclose her as the harsh cloud of fog and ice particles swept quickly over the boat, glazing it completely in a veneer of smooth clear ice.

As Brad strained to guide the two girls back along the side of the cabin, his foot slipped on the now icy deck. Both his feet then suddenly went out from underneath him and he fell backwards over the side of the railing. He managed to grip one hand onto the rail just as his body went over and his feet splashed into the roiling sea.

Romy rushed at him and grabbed his other arm with both her gloved hands, but his body weighed too much for her to pull him back up.

She saw the fear in his face and thought she was going to lose him to the sea just as Anik's dark, bare hand reached over her, grabbed Brad's wrist and pulled him back up and over the railing onto the boat.

"He'll be okay," Anik reassured Romy, but she could still see the concern in her father's face as he sat slumped and breathing heavily on the slippery deck.

Vance suddenly appeared out of the thick fog, carefully making his way over to them along the icy deck, and Romy could see fear in his face, too.

"Daddy, be careful," Tamika called out to him from behind Romy.

Vance nodded and he helped Anik lift Brad and usher him slowly to the back of the boat.

The two girls waited on the icy deck, clinging to each other, not daring to move, until Anik appeared again and with his strong arms he guided them back and around into the shelter of the little cabin.

"Are you okay, dad?" Romy asked her father.

Brad nodded, but Romy could see he was still shaken.

Vance kneeled down next to him and put his hand on his shoulder.

"You do a lot better in the sand than you do on the ice, my friend," he said, trying to make light of it.

"I guess so," Brad said quietly.

Romy looked over at Tamika and she could see the concern her friend had for her father too.

We'd better thank Santa for sending us Anik, Romy whispered to Tamika. Tamika nodded her head in agreement.

"We'll let this fog front pass," Anik said, "and then we'll still reach land in another couple hours."

His cousin held the throttle at a low, steady speed that kept the boat just barely moving forward so that if they hit an iceberg, it would just be a small bump. They could see little directly in front of them, but the large white shapes moved slowly past the sides of the boat like huge ghosts floating through the dense fog.

The seven of them stood together in the small cabin, staring intently out the front windshield, even though they could see nothing but the white wall of dense, cold fog in front of them. The ice was growing thicker on the surfaces of the boat.

Romy looked up at Brad's and Vance's faces. She no longer saw fear, but their brows were still tight with concern. They're dads again, not soldiers, she thought, and when her father suddenly looked back down at her, she felt warmth from his smile, even though she could tell he was forcing it to reassure her that all was okay.

She didn't want to lose him to the dangers of the arctic.

She wondered for a second if she should tell him that they could turn around and head back home. The trip might be too much for him. She started to speak, but she caught herself when her fingers wrapped around her mother's locket in her pocket.

No, she had to bring her mother and father together. They had to say good-bye. Her dad would thank her for it in the long run.

She hoped.

She smiled back at him and gave him a gentle high five, hoping she was reassuring him.

Please, Santa, watch out for us, she thought.

As quickly as the fog had arrived, it disappeared, and the seven of them suddenly found themselves looking out across a calmer ocean, still dark and cold, but with the tips of the waves sparkling in the dancing light of the almost full moon. The icebergs were seemed crisp and bright white as they floated by.

Thank you, Santa, Romy said, too quietly for anyone else to hear.

Anik's cousin pushed the throttle back up to full speed and the bow of the boat lifted again as it headed for the shoreline off to the northeast. The closer they got, the more the rough edge of the glacier, white in the moon light, seemed to rise up and Romy could see how rough the surface of the snowy ice was as it stretched back up in a sweeping arc between the two mountains on either side of it.

The glacier was huge, and the air cracked loudly as large chunks of ice broke off and splashed into the cold sea every few minutes as the boat approached the enormous wall of ice.

As they reached the edge of it, the boat turned sideways to dock up against one low ledge of ice jutting out into the sea. Quickly Anik and his son roused the dogs, lifted the wooden sleds over onto the ice and prepared the harnesses for the Huskies. Anik's cousin carried the supplies out and with Brad and Vance's help loaded them into the back of the large sleds.

The two girls carefully stepped off the boat and onto the ice while Anik set the dogs into the harnesses on one sled and Qannik did the same on the other.

"I'll be back here at noon in six days," Anik's cousin shouted to him. "May the spirits keep you safe."

"In this and the other world," Anik shouted back at him and then turned to the girls and their fathers.

"Quick!" Anik said to them. "This ice could break off any moment."

Romy and her dad quickly nestled into the warm caribou fur that lined Anik's sled while Tamika and Vance settled into Qannik's. Anik snapped his whip once in the air and immediately the dogs yipped and started pulling the sleds slowly up the glacier.

"We need to cross the glacier before we camp tonight on the ice field," Anik said to Romy and Brad. "The glacier can shift during the night and we don't need to find ourselves at the bottom of a hundred foot crevasse in the morning."

"No, we don't," Brad said.

A movement in the sky caught Romy's eye and she looked up into the dark sky in front of them. A huge white snowy owl was circling above the ice, two hundred feet in front of them, as if it was waiting for them to catch up. Like the snowy mountains and the iceberg, it too glowed in the light of the moon.

Romy pointed at the white bird and Anik nodded his head slowly and smiled.

"This is a good omen," he said. "The spirits have sent him to guide us to meet your mothers."

Thank you, Santa, Romy whispered.

Chapter Six

"We'll camp here tonight," Anik said as he pulled back on the sled's reigns and his dozen Huskies came to a stop on the edge of the ice field. Qannik's dogs and sleigh pulled up next to him.

Romy's eyes had gotten used to the moonlight during their long afternoon trip across the glacier, and now as she looked around at the vast expanse of the white ice field in front of her – perfectly flat and seemingly stretching out forever -- she began to feel at home in the eerie glow of this new world where everything seemed so different.

Above her the snowy owl made one final loop over the sleds before flying off to find shelter for the night.

Romy pulled the caribou wrap off her, climbed out of the sled and tightened the cords of her parka hood so that only her nose and eyes were visible through the hole in the red nylon. As she walked over to the dogs Anik had released from their harnesses, the loud creak of her boots on the cold snow reverberated in the air around her.

"That's Blizzard, my lead dog," Anik said, pointing to the largest Husky, "and that's Wizard, my son's alpha dog.

Romy called out their names, but the dogs were milling around anxiously, expecting to be fed, and Blizzard only passed his nose briefly across the tips of Romy's gloves as he paced back and forth restlessly.

Brad and Vance had started setting up the bright orange tent that they and their daughters would sleep in. Anik and his son had their own tent and Brad watched Qannik cutting blocks of snow and erecting a wall around the tent to keep the wind out if a storm came up.

Once their tent was up, Brad and Vance started cutting and piling up snow blocks around their tent too.

In the neatly cut rectangle in the ice cap that Anik had cut the blocks from, Qannik was carefully placing much of the food supply they'd brought with them for themselves and for the dogs. Anik told Brad and Vance this would lighten their load, and they'd have the food right here for them on their way back home.

After the dogs had been fed, Anik and Qannik crawled into the tent with the fathers and girls and Anik began heating up a meal for them all on a small gas burner.

"Whale meat is good for you," Anik said to them as he cut strips from a flank he unwrapped and warmed them in the boiling water. "It makes your body warm, strong, healthy."

Warm is good, Romy thought.

He passed the warmed strips of meat around to the fathers and the girls and then cut each of them a quarter of a flat bread loaf he took from his food pack. Anik and Qannik ate their whale meat raw.

After they'd finished eating, Brad pulled his sleeve back to look at his watch.

"With everything always this same dim light, it's hard to tell what time it is," he said.

He looked down at his thick watch with its many buttons. It was a military model and Romy knew it had been very expensive, too expensive for her to replace with a better one as a Christmas gift for him.

Brad started tapping his watch with his fingers.

"My watch isn't working," he said with surprise.

"There's almost no time up here," Anik said quietly. "Don't worry about it. It'll work again back in Ilulliset."

"It must be the polar magnetic fields," Vance offered.

"Maybe," Romy said.

She looked over at Tamika and Tamika winked at her.

After Anik and his son had left for their own tent, the fathers and daughters lay their sleeping bags out and squeezed down into them. Brad reached over, pulled his backpack to him and unzipped a pocket on the side of it.

"I have a little treat in here for us," he said.

Romy had seen him buy three large chocolate bars at the hotel, but didn't say anything then so she could pretend to be surprised whenever he brought them out. She knew he'd be storing them for the trip.

"Wait a minute," he said.

He slowly lifted his arm up, straight out in front of him. He was holding a brightly colored, red knitted scarf in his fingers, delicately, as if it were a treasure.

"This wasn't here when we left," he said. "It's exactly like the ones mom always knitted for me. How did it get here?"

Romy looked over at Tamika.

"Mom probably wanted you to be warm on your trip up here," Romy said to him.

"This doesn't make sense," Brad said.

"No. It doesn't," Vance added, but he pulled his own pack toward him and opened the side pouch.

"Brad," he said.

"What, Vance?" Brad asked.

"I've got one too."

The next morning Romy was the first to step out of their tent. She saw Anik and Qannik had already taken down their tent and were preparing the dogs for the day's journey, but the Huskies were pacing back and forth, whimpering and glancing back behind Romy. Blizzard and Wizard were scampering around, too, their eyes on the horizon behind Romy, trying to avoid being harnessed by Anik and Qannik.

Romy turned to look behind her and understood.

No more than a hundred feet away a great white Arctic wolf, much larger than any of the Huskies, was staring at her.

In the light of the moon she could make out the clear eyes and shiny black pupils of the majestic animal as he held her in his gaze without flinching. He's looking right through me, Romy thought.

He's here for food, Romy thought, and realized why the Huskies were so frantic, even the two lead dogs, to find themselves stalked by such a predator. With its stark white, thick coat, powerful shoulders and unwavering gaze the lone wolf seemed like Arctic royalty to Romy, but as she dared to stare back into its penetrating eyes, she felt its presence was not really that of a predator, but of a guide.

Has Santa sent you, she wondered.

The wolf turned slowly and marched off to the north several paces before pausing and looking back over its muscular shoulder at Romy.

"He wants to lead us!" Romy shouted over to Anik.

"So I see," Anik said. "Now we have two spirit guides," he added and pointed up into the night sky at the large snowy owl circling above them again.

The sled dogs had all settled down now and were standing patiently as Anik and Qaniik put on their harnesses.

"On our third night we'll be in the spirits' place," Anik called over to Romy, "where Qannik and I have been with his mother, and where you will be with yours."

Brad and Vance had come out of the tent behind Romy and she turned to look at them and smiled as she pointed first to the wolf and then to the owl, both so white in the moonlight, but she saw only concern on the fathers' faces.

"It's okay. They're just waiting for us. We'd better pack up and get going," Romy said to her father.

"Right," Brad said and turned and bent over to go back into the tent. Vance followed him.

Tamika, who had been standing behind them, held her orange gloved hand out in front of her so Romy could give her a quick high-five.

"We're close!" she said.

"Yes," Romy said to her friend.

Romy was nestled warmly under the caribou skin and sat back between her father's legs as the sled traveled north through the luminescent white landscape. She leaned back against her father's chest, comforted by the thought that soon she, and her father, would see her mother again and once again they would be a complete family, even if only for a moment.

At least she and her dad would be able to locate her mother, she thought, or at least know where she was, rather than having to think she was gone altogether, suddenly and mysteriously, from their lives.

After this, they would always know where she was.

Romy couldn't wait to watch her father's expression when he saw her – he'd be like a child opening his first present of the Christmas morning -- and as the sled moved quickly to their destination she mused over his response. He'd be surprised, she knew, maybe even a little disbelieving at first, but in the end he'd be comforted, warmed even, by whatever words her mother would say to him. It would be a joy.

She couldn't wait.

That night, after they'd set up their tents and Anik had warmed their whale meat dinner for them, the girls and their fathers prepared their sleeping bags for the night. Anik had been out taking care of the dogs, but he came back to their tent and called to them through the nylon flap.

Brad opened lifted the flap and Anik motioned him out. Vance and the girls followed him out to see what Anik wanted.

"Look," Anik said and pointed out across the white landscape.

Just above the ice field Romy could see a white trail of ice particles and light snow being blown slowly but steadily across the surface of the white world.

"Storm's coming," Anik said. "Could be a bad one."

Romy looked up into the night sky. There were no clouds above her, just the brilliant moon just above the horizon, a few sparkling stars bright enough to be visible despite the light of the moon and, to the north, a curtain of greenish lights slowly weaving back and forth in front of the North Star. The Aurora Borealis. The polar spirits.

How's he know there's going to be a storm, Romy wondered. The night looked so calm and peaceful to her. Except for that lightly blowing snow, of course. It already seemed to be moving a little more quickly across the ice cap's surface, just in the few minutes since she'd been outside. Okay, that's how he knows, she thought.

"We'll need to make the snow walls higher around the tents tonight," Anik said. "Just in case."

Brad and Vance joined the two guides and started to cut more snow blocks from the ice field and lift them onto the low wall they'd already built around each tent. Romy and Tamika went back inside.

"This is exciting!" Romy said.

"This is scary," Tamika replied.

"Really?"

"Look," Tamika said, "We've only got food enough for one more day north and to get back to where we stored the rest of it last night. What if we get stranded in a storm? We won't be able to go any further. We'll never get to see our moms, never get to have our dads say good-bye to them."

"That sounds awfully logical, Tamika," Romy said.

"Oh. I guess it does. Maybe it's just time for you to talk to Santa," Tamika said.

"Right."

The wind now sounded louder to Romy and she could see it starting to wrinkle the sides of the tent.

For the first time since they'd left Ilulliset, Romy felt herself shiver with the cold, like there was a chill in her chest.

Brad and Vance came back into the tent after building the snow wall almost to the height of the tent. Their eyebrows, their eyelashes and Brad's moustache were all coated with ice crystals from the wind and the cold and the blowing snow.

"It's snowing pretty good out there now," Brad said.

Does this mean we're getting closer to our mothers, Romy wondered, or does it mean something has gone all wrong up here.

"Look, Romy," Brad said, "I think we may need to turn around and go home. This storm could be too much for us."

The sides of the tent had started flapping noisily, like a ship's mainsails rippling in a heavy sea storm.

"We're both so proud of each of you," Vance aid. "You've led us up here this far with no fear, without giving up, even convincing Brad and I to go on when we didn't want to be convinced. But now, it's no longer safe for us up here, wherever up here really is."

Romy started to cry, not because she thought that would make them change their minds, but because she thought they might be right.

She looked over at Tamika and she was crying too. Romy felt guilty, as if she had somehow let her down too.

Santa, where are you, Romy thought.

For the next two days the storm raged against the little tents. Anik and his son and Brad and Vance had to keep digging out the space between the snow walls and the tents because it filled in every few hours with the fierce winds and the heavy snow that went on and on with no end.

Anik cooked them meals three times a day, but even after cutting back on the size of their portions, by the end of the second day they all knew they were close to running out of their rations.

Every time Romy peeked outside through the flap of the tent to see if the storm was lessening, all she could see was a screen of white particles rushing past her as the wind blinded her entire world with the thick snow. There was no ground to be seen, no horizon, no sky, just the fast moving wall of white right in front of her. This was too many snowflakes, she thought, way too many.

With no reference points at all in their world – no space, no time, and everything just white – they all began to sleep in fitful naps, and as they went longer and longer without food, they began to spend more and more time in their warm bags sleeping, no longer fitfully, but deeply, as their bodies gave in to the lack of food.

At one point Romy woke up and looked out her bag to find her father staring at her from the little opening in his own sleeping bag.

"You're all I have," he whispered to her, and then his eyelids closed and his head slowly went back down into the bag.

There was no movement in the other sleeping bags in the tent and Romy thought this might be the end. The end of her family, she thought, but by then she was too tired, too weak to even cry.

She hadn't seen or heard from Anik or Qannik for hours, and she worried what might be happening to the dogs too.

She could barely keep herself awake, and she kept pressing her thumbnail into the palm of her hand inside her glove to try to keep herself alert. She read about that once on Wikipedia. It was the only thought she could keep in her mind and she was afraid that if she let go of that thought and went to sleep again, she might not wake up.

With the heavy snow outside, there was almost no light inside the tent and she strained to keep her eyes open as she looked around at the three nylon bags around her. The wind was still deafening as it howled around the tent, and Romy struggled to try to tell if there was any lessening of its force.

There wasn't.

She strained to keep concentrating on the rise and fall of the noisy gusts of wind so she could keep herself aawake, but she also began to sense some other "noise" behind the howling of the wind. It was not a worldly noise, but it was something she could definitely hear and it was getting stronger.

Suddenly she thought she recognized it.

"Santa?" she called out, quietly.

Chapter Seven

Romy's vision had gone all snowy for a minute and she had to squint to bring the world in front of her back into focus.

Where was she now, she wondered.

There was a reindeer in front of her, and he seemed enormous with his ten point antlers. He looked back around over his shoulder at Romy while two elves carried a sleeping Tamika to the sleigh behind him.

The snow owl circled above him and the full moon made the white landscape glow. There was no storm here.

Romy took all this in, trying to understand it as her mind began to come into focus, just as her vision had.

Brad and Vance were already in the seat of the sleigh, sitting with their heads thrown back and their eyes shut. The two elves had settled Tamika in next to Vance and they leaned her head against his shoulder. Her eyes too stayed tightly closed.

Romy didn't know if they were all still asleep. Or worse.

One elf beckoned Romy with one tiny curled finger and she walked forward, almost trancelike, across the snow. The elf helped her up into the seat of the sleigh next to Brad and then sat down on the floor in front of her. The other elf jumped in and sat next to him. Romy was surprised at how happy they looked. Maybe things weren't that bad.

Romy looked over and could now see from the slow rise and fall of their chests that Brad, Vance and Tamika were breathing. I don't know what I would have done, Romy thought, if my father had been taken from me too.

"Home, Donner!" one elf yelled out and the sleigh bolted forward into the night.

Romy's eyes were now able to focus sharply on the elves, the sleigh and her father's face next to her, but when she looked out toward the snow covered horizon, everything still looked blurry, as if the world itself was still out of focus at its fringes.

Looking off into the distance like that made her dizzy, and she brought her gaze back to the huge reindeer in front of her galloping across the snow.

Romy realized she couldn't tell if they had been traveling all through the night or if they had just arrived in a minute, but all of a sudden in front of her she saw a large wooden cottage stretched out across the snow. The tiny windows glowed warmly with the first light, inside, that Romy had seen in days.

The sled pulled up to the cottage, Donner snorted twice and shook his magnificent head and the one elf who appeared to be in charge led Romy up to the front door.

"Don't worry. We'll take care of your dad and friends," he said and turned back to the sleigh.

Romy stared at the beautiful wreath that covered the whole top half of the door and then noticed a little silver bell to the right with a leather strap hanging down from its gong. She reached over and pulled it back sharply once against the bell. Nothing happened. She pulled it again and it rang.

The door slowly opened and a short, plump woman with white, white hair stood smiling at Romy.

"We're glad you've arrived," she said.

"Where are we?" Romy asked her.

"Well, we're sort of in between," the old woman said.

Romy felt comforted by the woman's kind face, but when she looked into her eyes, it was like looking off at the horizon from the sleigh. She couldn't quite bring the woman's eyes into focus. Romy didn't feel so much dizzy as just not quite present.

The woman held out her hand and led Romy into a large room warmed by a fireplace over on the far wall. A long wooden table with wooden chairs was to her left and soft upholstered chairs and a sofa were clustered on her right.

The room was softly lit by candles and Romy suddenly felt warm and happy and alert as the woman led her over to the sofa, but when Romy tried to look at the log walls of the room, they too would not quite come into focus. There was something about the edges of this world, she thought.

"Are Anik and Qannik okay?" Romy asked the woman after they both had sat down on the sofa. The cushions were so deep Romy felt like she was being folded into a soft, warm cloud and she had to reach down and touch them with her fingers just to make sure they were real.

"They will be fine," the woman said. "When they wake, they will hardly know anything has happened."

"And the dogs?" Romy asked.

"They will be fine, too. And your father and Tamika and her father are all being taken care of right now. They'll be awake again soon."

"Why am I still awake then?" Romy asked.

"Because you are the strongest one," the woman said. "Maybe I should say you are the wisest one, but in life it is wisdom that produces strength. And, you believe. Would you like some hot chocolate?"

"Yes, please," Romy said. "Is Santa here?"

"Of course he is," the white haired woman replied. "Soon he will give you the gift you've been waiting for. You did well, you know, getting here."

She patted the back of Romy's hand and then rose to go get the hot chocolate.

In a minute she came back with the warm drinks for them both and a plate of sugar cookies full of white chocolate sprinkles carved into tiny snowflakes.

As Romy bit into one of the cookies, she suddenly became aware of her mother's presence. She wasn't quite sure exactly where, but she knew her mother was somehow now nearby.

"It is time," the old woman said. It was as if she too knew Romy's mother was near.

The woman stood and gave her hand to Romy so she could lead her across the room to a wooden door, hand carved with delicate figures of elves and reindeer. She opened the door slowly and bright light flowed out from the room and covered the woman and Romy.

The light felt warm to Romy and it felt, well, happy, she thought, but it made the whole room out of focus, just like the horizon had been. As she entered the room in front of the old woman, Romy could not see any walls anywhere and it seemed like the white light of the room went on forever, even though she felt contained in an immediate space.

"Welcome to the North Pole, Romy," a deep voice somewhere in front of Romy said.

As Romy stepped slowly forward into the light, she began to see the outline of a large man and as she moved closer she recognized the red suit and the white beard and full head of long white hair.

"Thank you," she said. "Thank you for everything."

"Please bring in her father and the other two," the man said to the old woman, who was now standing right behind Romy.

"Yes, dear," she said.

In a moment Tamika, Brad and Vance came in, hand in hand, led by the woman. Tamika was smiling softly, and Romy had never seen her eyes so alive, so happy.

Brad and Vance stood next to each other in silence and Romy realized their minds had not come into focus yet. They looked calm, but quite awed by everything.

"I know you each have a gift to give your mothers," the deep voice said to the girls, "and I know you fathers have your gift for them too. Your love," he added as he spoke to Brad and Vance.

He raised his hand slowly until his red sleeve stretched far up into the light, and suddenly a woman's fingers reached down to be guided by his hand to the floor in front of Romy. He reached up a second time and Tamika's mother descended from above as well.

"Mommy!" Romy said and ran over to her mother's arms.

Tamika ran into her mother's arms and Brad and Vance stepped closer to the women, but they paused to let their daughters remain by themselves within their mothers' arms.

Romy stepped back and reached into her pocket for the crinkled paper that held her mother's locket.

"Merry Christmas, mama," she said as she placed her gift in her mother's open palm.

"Thank you, my dear," her mother said to her. "And Merry Christmas to you, too. Those charms look good on you." She pointed to the silver bracelet around Romy's left wrist.

Tamika's mother had taken her locket from her daughter and was fastening it with Tamika's help around her neck.

"I brought daddy, and Tamika did too," Romy said to her mother "so we could all be a family again while we said good-bye."

"We will always be a family," Romy's mother said. "Life is more than just the world you came from so you could see us here. We'll stay a family 'til you return again. Just as we are now. And forever."

"You have given each other your gifts," Santa said, "and I have now given you your gift, Romy, because you believed. But all of you have the gift of love for each other, and that is the greatest gift of all." He looked carefully at one girl and then the other and Romy thought she saw him wink. "And all of you, all of you now believe. Merry Christmas. Merry Christmas to two beautiful families."

Brad and Vance were nodding their heads in agreement. They had stayed back, tears in their eyes, watching as the girls and their mothers hugged, but now they joined Romy and Tamika and their mothers, and the two families hugged for one final moment.

"Now it is time to go," Romy's mother said, and she let herself be lifted up by the hand at the end of the red sleeve back into the light above.

Tamika's mother followed.

"Come," the white haired woman said and she guided Romy and Tamika and their fathers back out into the front room.

"Bundle up now," the woman told them as she handed them their scarves and gloves and parkas from the wooden hooks by the front door.
"Donner's waiting with a sled to take you back."

Once the four of them were ready, she opened the front door and they saw Donner hitched to the sleigh out on the cold snow. The two elves stood waiting next to the huge reindeer.

"Are you two okay?" Romy called into the smaller tent.

Anik poked his head out, a big smile on his face.

"That was the best sleep," he said, "and I dreamed of my wife the whole time, just as if she were right here with us." He stuck his head out further through the tent's flap and looked around. "The storm's passed. If we hurry, we won't starve to death before we get back to the food we stored."

"There's no hurry," Brad said. "Look."

He'd opened up the food locker on the back of one sled and Anik saw it was full of fresh whale meat, enough for them and for the dogs.

"How is that possible?" he asked.

"As we say -- where we're from -- Merry Christmas," Romy said.

"Ah! The spirits do live," Anik responded.

Chapter Eight

Romy looked out through the window of the room in the nursing home and saw that the first snowflakes of the Christmas season had started to fall.

"It's time," Romy said to her friend in the bed next to hers.

"Yes, it is," Tamika replied.

"We did well," Romy said.

"Yes, we did. It's hard to believe we haven't seen our moms for almost eighty-five years," Tamika said. She reached her thin arm across the space between the two beds and ran her index finger across Romy's charm bracelet before clasping Romy's hand in her own.

Romy smiled and looked over at the ornament mounted in the glass case sitting on the dresser next to the window.

"Do you suppose he still has his ornament?" Romy asked.

"Donovan? Of course he does," Tamika said.

"You know, when he first came into our shop with his mother all those many years ago, I would never thought he could be so wise. He was so young."

"He sure was a handsome little fellow," Tamika said, "but until he saw the ornament, I thought he was just another child who'd come into our store for some Christmas spirit and to buy some Christmas goodies."

“But when he looked at the ornament and shouted out, ‘That’s Greenland!’ we knew, didn’t we?” Romy said.

“And then, when he told us how proud our mothers must be of us, because we opened the Snowflake Christmas Shoppe, it was like Santa himself was speaking to us.”

“Donovan believed,” Romy said.

“But how could he have possibly known we’d already seen our moms. And, that we’d see them again, like we will today?” Tamika said.

“There are some things that people just know. Especially children. That’s why we opened the gift shop, no? So that children could know, so that they could believe.”

“You know, sometimes I wished we’d opened our shop much earlier…instead of me spending all those years as a nurse and you as a teacher,” Tamika mused.

"Yes, but we didn't have any money, remember? We may have had the gift of believing in Christmas, but we didn't have the gift of cash, then," Romy said.

"Donovan's mother was a nurse, just like me."

"She was a good woman," Romy said. "Just like you," she added and squeezed Tamika's hand.

"Her name was Christina. She worked at Litchfield Woods, another nursing home. Connecticut, I think. I always remember the name because it sounded like Sherwood Forest to me, and Donovan was like a little Robin Hood. Do you think we should have given him the ornament from my tree?"

"Of course, we should have," Romy said. "He was a special child. And we've always had the other one." Romy pointed at the ornament in the glass case on the dresser, the one Romy herself had found on her tree that night so long before.

"That really was the best Christmas gift we could have given any of the children who visited our shop, wasn't it?" Tamika said as she gazed at the lone ornament in the glass case.

"It was, and Donovan's done something special with it, I'm sure. It is quite magic, you know. He'll have shown others how to believe, just as we did," Romy said and looked across at Tamika with a broad smile. "He'll have made his own family of believers, just as we did in the store."

Romy looked back again at the face on the ornament, startled.

"Is it me or is Santa suddenly smiling there?" she asked.

"I think so. And look!" Tamika said and pointed out the window of their room. "More snowflakes too."

"The Christmas season has begun," Romy said. "Are you ready?"

"Yes."

"Are you excited?"

"Yes! Our next adventure."

"Then let's go," Romy said, and she and Tamika closed their eyes.

Outside their room the day nurse was making her way back to the nurses' station at the end of the hall when she saw a bright light suddenly appear from underneath the door to Romy and Tamika's room. It flowed out from under the narrow slit between the bottom of the door and the shiny linoleum floor and then spread throughout the hallway, filling the space up with a soft fuzzy light, like gentle snow.

The nurse stopped in her tracks. She felt warm in the light, and happy, she thought, but she didn't know why, and she heard a deep, soothing man's voice in the room, but she couldn't make out what he was saying.

Then the light stopped, and the hallway returned to what seemed to the nurse to now be only a dim glow from the fluorescent lights running along the ceiling. She walked slowly over to the door of Romy and Tamika's room and carefully turned the knob.

Romy and Tamika felt themselves rising up through the gentle snow falling outside the nursing home, guided by the hand of the man dressed in red. As they rose higher and higher, the snow slowly became a warm white light, and high above them in the distance, they saw two silhouettes.

Romy and Tamika looked below them and saw the red sleeve had stopped rising with them and was now lifted up, pointing in the direction of the glowing figures above them. The two of them kept rising slowly and the two figures above them began to come into focus, more and more, until the girls recognized their mothers.

As they neared their mothers and stretched their arms out to hug them, they could see the sparkles of light reflected from the lockets around their mothers' necks.

"Romy!"

"Tamika!"

The four figures, mother and daughter, mother and daughter, merged into each other as they hugged as one in the glow of the light that enveloped them.

"Welcome home," Tamika's mother said.

"Yes, welcome back home," Romy's mother added. "You both did so well in that world."

"You two have always kept believing," Tamika's mother said. "And you helped so many children believe. Your Snowflake Christmas Shoppe was as magic as your trip to the North Pole, so many years ago." She paused for a second. "Or was that just yesterday?" she asked Romy's mother.

"Both," Romy's mother answered, smiling.

"We are family," Tamika's mother said.

"You knew that when children believe," Romy's mother said, "your world and our world stay connected, stay family."

"Anik knew that too, didn't he?" Romy asked.

"Yes, he did," her mother answered. "We met his wife back then. And we've met him, too. We're all, really, family."

"Let's go see your dads," Tamika's mother said and held out her hand to guide the girls farther up into the light.

The nurse slowly opened the door to the room, slightly frightened, slightly excited, not knowing what she'd see.

On the beds the two women's bodies lay peacefully with their eyes closed. Each had a soft, quiet smile on the lips as if the women had both been totally contented.

How sweet, the nurse thought, and how sad that two of her favorite residents had passed, but she was deeply pleased that they must have gone so comfortably.

She looked around the room, saw the snow falling heavily outside the window and then her eyes stopped at the glass case on the dresser.

The women had often told her the ornament was what prompted them to start their Christmas gift shop in the first place, and the nurse had often marveled at the delicate brush strokes that created Santa's face and the mountains framing the sheer white ice field.

She always had felt happy, somehow, when she stood admiring the ornament through the clear glass of the case.

But now the case was empty.

She thought she knew why. The ornament was now ready for another child in the world who believed.

Made in the USA
Middletown, DE
04 September 2020